MY SISTER IS A UNICORN

BY ELAINE HENEY

Books for kids

My sister is a unicorn series

For adults

Equine Listenology Guide
Equine Listenology Workbook
Equine Listenology Journal
Equine Listenology Diary
Ozzie, the Story of a Young Horse
Conversations with the Horse
The Horse Riders Training Journal
Groundwork Training Journal
Liberty Training Journal

Online horse courses for adults:

www.greyponyfilms.com

iPhone & Android Horse Apps:

www.horsestridesapp.com
www.rideableapp.com
www.dressagehero.com
www.greyponyfilms.com

FOR CLODAGH & CIARA & EVERYONE WHO BELIEVES IN UNICORNS & MAGIC

THIS BOOK BELONGS TO:

'Oh dearie me, perhaps you're right
You must have got an awful fright
She's a little girl, a unicorn filly
I've got the perfect name, let's call her Tilly!'

A smell descended through the room
'She's done a fart, like bad perfume
'Quick, open the windows let in some air
This room stinks and it's in my hair!'

'You're my big sister' the unicorn said
She gave me a big sloppy kiss on my head
'Ugh that's gross, there's slime on my face'
'I love you' said Tilly, 'now let's have a race!'

My sister is a unicorn, it's weird but true
I go to the bathroom she goes to the loo
The farrier and the vet are her new best friends
Her hooves are perfect and her tail never ends

She uses a bucket to eat her lunch
She loves oats and apples and treats for brunch
Her mane is pink and her tail is blue
Her teeth are large and she cleans them too

We go to school on the bumpity bus
I learn to read, Tilly learns to jump...

When the teachers are not
looking we gallop off fast
We jump all the ditches
and the fields fly past...

We find ourselves in a swimming pool
And splash about forgetting school
Tilly shouts 'let's try the slide!'
'Crack' it goes, it's time to hide!

We look around, there's a riding school
With a dressage competition
'let's enter, it looks cool!'
Tilly dazzles with no bridle or bit
She wins first prize, then it's time to split

Tilly is hungry so we've got to stop
She does a poo then back off we trot
We find an orchard with apples galore
We munch them for dinner,
then have even more

We go to the airport,
and jump on a plane
I'm drinking juice,
Tillys drinking champagne

'Stow away your bags
in the overhead lockers
Hey unicorn — you need to get
off the plane, you're bonkers!'

My sister and I are removed from the flight
We canter through security out into the night

'We've got to go home,
it's time for bed'
'Alright' said Tilly,
'which way shall we head?'

We gallop through the fields all the way back home
My parents were mad cos I didn't answer my phone

'Where were you all day,
we were worried sick?'
'Long story' I said,
'we were taking the mick'

'Get up to your rooms,
you're both in big trouble.
We'll decide exactly what to do
with you two in the morning'

We trot back upstairs,
big smiles on our faces
Our secrets are safe,
we've covered our bases

My sister is a unicorn
And it's very weird to some
But I love her a lot
And there's lots more trouble to come!

READ MORE!

ENJOY THE ENTIRE CIARA + TILLY THE UNICORN BOOK SERIES

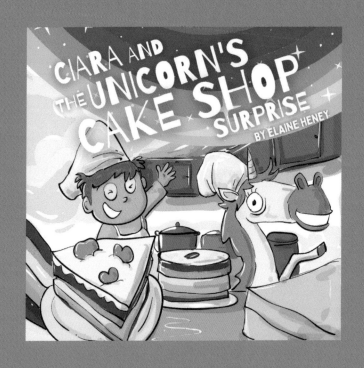

Enjoy our new book for kids ages 6-11

THANK YOU FOR READING THIS BOOK. IF YOU ENJOYED THIS BOOK PLEASE LEAVE A REVIEW!

MORE BOOKS IN THIS UNICORN SERIES ARE WAITING FOR YOU!

Printed in Great Britain
by Amazon